BEANY

Wakes Up for Christmas

Weekly Reader Children's Book Club Presents

BEANY

Story by Lisa Bassett
Pictures by Jeni Bassett

Wakes Up
for Christmas

G.P. Putnam's Sons • New York

To the memory of Grampy,
Dr. George R. Crisler

This book is a presentation of Weekly Reader Books. Weekly Reader
Books offers book clubs for children from preschool through high
school. For further information write to: **Weekly Reader Books,**
4343 Equity Drive, Columbus, Ohio 43228.

Published by arrangement with The Putnam & Grosset Group.
Weekly Reader is a trademark of Field Publications.
Printed in the United States of America.

Published simultaneously in Canada
Printed in Italy by New Interlitho S.P.A.
Library of Congress Cataloging-in-Publication Data
Bassett, Lisa.   Beany wakes up for Christmas.
Summary: Scamp Squirrel gets everything ready for Christmas to
surprise Beany when he wakes up for the occasion.
[1. Bears—Fiction. 2. Squirrels—Fiction. 3. Christmas—Fiction]
I. Bassett, Jeni, ill. II. Title.   PZ7.B2933Bi   1988b   [E]   88-18195
ISBN 0-399-21668-5
First impression

Before Beany Bear climbed into bed
for his long winter's nap, he sent a note
to Scamp Squirrel.
The note said:

Dear Scamp,

Please don't forget to wake me up for

Christmas this year. I have a present for you.

Your friend,

Beany

"Oh, I *won't* forget," said Scamp when he got the note. "Oh, no! This year I will give Beany a surprise. I will decorate a tree and also fix a Christmas feast!"

Scamp marked the days off on his calendar. On
Christmas Eve, he went skipping down the path
to Beany's house. As he went along, he looked
for a Christmas tree, but all the fir trees were
much too big for a small squirrel to manage.
"I will have to settle for a bush," said Scamp.
He cut down a little bush and dragged it
on his sled to Beany's house.

First, Scamp checked on Beany. He was sleeping
soundly. Then Scamp began to unpack the dusty
boxes of decorations. The lights were all in a
tangle. Scamp tried to untie the wires, but
somehow the knots only got tighter.

Scamp put the whole wad of lights on top
of the bush.

"The tree will look prettier when I put on the
Christmas balls," he said. But Scamp
fell over the boxes, and the bright red and
green balls rolled under the sofa, the chair,
and bumped into the corners.

"Well, the Christmas balls do not matter much,"
said Scamp. "I will just add some tinsel, and
then I will start the feast."

For some reason, the tinsel stayed in a clump.
When Scamp put it on the bush, it hung
all together on one branch.

Scamp stood back and looked at the bush.
"Humm…Beany *will* be surprised when he
sees this Christmas tree! But now I must
make a feast. I will fix Beany's favorite
Honey Punch and then Pumpkin Seed Pie."
And with one last look at the Christmas bush,
Scamp rushed into the kitchen to get to work.

He pulled out the big cookbook and several jars
of Beany's best honey. "Ah...three jars of
golden honey...a carton of ice cream...a dash
of this and two pawfuls of that. Now for the
ginger soda!" Scamp mixed the punch with a big
spoon and took a taste. "Oh, my! What perfect
punch!" he cried, hopping up and down. The
empty jars and the soda bottle crashed to the floor.
"Now for the pie!" exclaimed Scamp.

Meanwhile, Beany snuggled deeper under the
covers. He was dreaming of Santa Claus. In
Beany's dream, Santa Claus kept clumping back
and forth on Beany's roof. The reindeer stamped
their hooves and jingled their bells.

Beany dreamed that Santa Claus came down the
chimney, but as he landed, he knocked over
a stack of logs with a bumpity, bump, BANG!

Beany started up in bed. "I heard something, and
I'm sure it wasn't Santa Claus." Beany sat very still
and strained his ears to listen. Suddenly he heard
a rattle and a thump and a scrape, scrape, scrape.
"What is in my house? Santa Claus doesn't sound
like *that*," gulped Beany. "It must be...it must
be a wild beast." Beany pulled the covers up
to his nose. "I wish Scamp were here. Scamp
would know what to do about a wild beast."

Just then, Beany saw Scamp trotting past his
window. "Scamp! Scamp!" cried Beany.
"Oh, Scamp, come in here quick!"
Scamp crawled in through the window.

"Beany, I was just going home to bed. It's not
Christmas morning yet. I was going to surprise
you!" said Scamp.

"But, Scamp! There is a wild beast in my house,"
cried Beany.

"Oh, dear, he must have slipped in as I went out the door," said Scamp. "And I know what he wants. That wild beast is after the Honey Punch!"

"Honey Punch? Did you make Honey Punch?" exclaimed Beany. "Oh, my, oh my, what if the wild beast drinks it all?"

"We have got to do *something*," said Scamp. "But
what? You are not an attacking sort of bear."

"No," Beany agreed.

"And I am too small. Why, a wild beast would
eat me like that! No, we will have to outwit
this beast."

Scamp began to pace across the bedroom.

Suddenly he grabbed Beany's sheets from the bed and began to cut holes in them.

"What are you doing?" cried Beany.

"We are going to frighten that beast away!"

Scamp threw a sheet over Beany and one
over himself. "A wild beast would never
stay in a haunted house!"
"Do I look like a ghost?" asked Beany.
"Exactly like a ghost," said Scamp.

They tiptoed through the door. Beany's sheet
was crooked, and he could only see out of one hole.
"Oh," whispered Beany. "There he is! There is the
wild beast."

"No," said Scamp. "That is your Christmas
tree. I decorated it."

"I...I guess the lights don't look right,"
said Beany.

"Well, we are looking for the beast, so come on."

They pattered to the kitchen door.

"We must make ghost noises," said Scamp.

"OOOOOOOOOOOOOHHH," said Beany.

"Ooooooooooooweeeeee," said Scamp, and they

poked their heads into the kitchen.

"Do you see the beast?" asked Scamp.

"I cannot see anything very well," replied
Beany, adjusting his sheet. Scamp peeked out
from under his sheet and peered around the
kitchen. "We did it! The beast is gone,"
said Scamp. "That wild beast was so scared
he didn't drink a drop of punch!"
"Haunting houses makes me thirsty," said Beany,
licking his lips.

"I suppose we could drink a little punch now,"
said Scamp. When they had finished the punch
and the Pumpkin Seed Pie, Scamp suddenly trotted
over to the window. "The sun is up. It is
Christmas morning and time to give presents!"

Beany opened the little package from Scamp.

"These are beautiful," said Beany politely,

"But what are they?"

"Mittens!" cried Scamp. "I made them myself."

"They are a bit small for my paws," said Beany.

"Oh, dear," said Scamp. "They fit *me* perfectly."

"But now open my present," said Beany. Scamp

tore into the package. "A tool kit!" exclaimed

Scamp. "Oh, Beany! Now I can fix anything!

I'll bet I could fix those lights," said Scamp,

pulling the hammer from the tool kit.

"No, no," said Beany with a yawn. "We will fix the

lights in the spring. I've got to go back to bed."

"Sleep well," said Scamp, as he went out the
door. "I will be back to wake you up in the spring."
Before Beany crawled into his bed, he looked at his
new mittens. "These mittens are just the thing!"
He slipped them over his ears. "If that wild
beast comes back, I won't hear a sound!"
Beany wrote another note to Scamp Squirrel:

Dear Scamp,

How did you know I needed mittens? You
are the best friend a bear could have.

Your friend,

Beany

P.S. Please don't wake me up *too* soon.